About this story:

Rumble the dragon just moved into his grandmother's old cave. He is working to turn the cave into a hotel. Then, he discovers he is not alone in his new home. A sly, old spider lives there too. Will Rumble let her stay?

Table of Contents

Book 2

Moves In

by Audra V. Pace

Illustrated by Lesley Danson

Based on text by Felicia Law
Editors: Jamie McCune & Samantha Schlemm
Book design: Katie Sears

First Edition 2012
10 9 8 7 6 5 4 3 2 1

Library of Congress Control Number: 2012944612

Rumble's First Guest

Rumble the dragon was busy.
He was cleaning the dust and the
spiders out of Granny's cave. Soon,
the cave would be a beautiful hotel.

Then Spider arrived,
Rumble's first unexpected
guest. Spider explained that
she was not a guest at all.
The cave was her home!

"Oh no it's not!"
Rumble roared. "This cave
is now a hotel. There are
no spiders allowed."

"Spiders make cobwebs," Rumble cried. "And cobwebs are messy. Guests will only stay in a clean hotel. Sorry, Spider, but you are out of luck."

Spider was angry. She was
very old and had lived in the
cave with Rumble's Granny for
many years. She did not want
to leave her home.

RUMBLE AND GRANNY

14

Guests Beware!

"I'll show you a mess!" Spider said.

She sat down outside of Rumble's cave and put up a sign to warn the guests:

Guests beware:
This hotel is DIRTY.
It has flies!

"How dare you say my hotel has flies?" Rumble exclaimed. He had not seen any flies since he moved in to Granny's cave. But he had seen cobwebs.

"There aren't any flies now, but there will be," Spider warned.

Spider explained that she could keep the flies away by catching them in her web. She said one little spider would be much cleaner than a million flies.

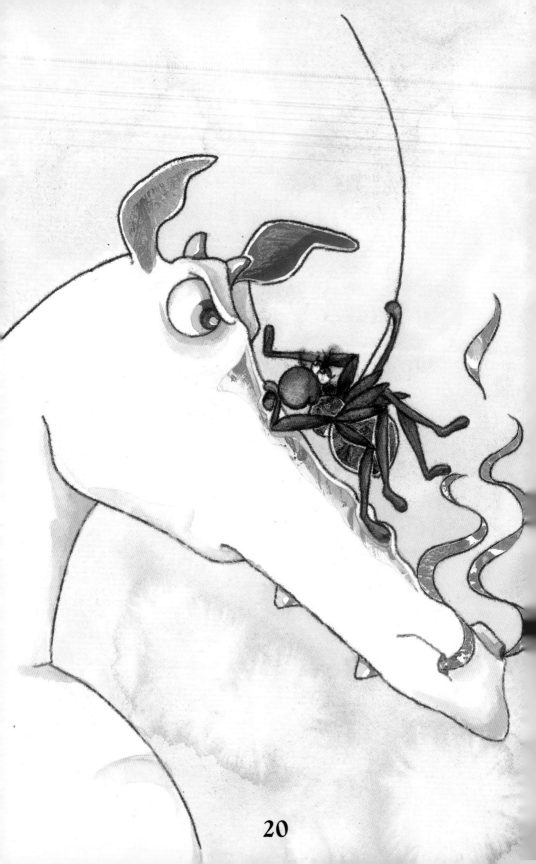

Rumble wasn't so sure. Spider told Rumble she wasn't just any spider. She was very old and very wise. She could see into the future, and she predicted Rumble's future was full of flies.

Rumble didn't like spiders, but he hated flies. He agreed to let Spider stay, but she would have to do her part.

Wise Old Spider

Since there were no flies
to trap, Spider agreed to work
as the hotel fortune teller.
She made a new sign:

Wise, old Spider will
tell your fortune!
Price: 1¢

Later, Rumble invited Spider back inside. He was happy to have her help, rather than none at all.

"Rumble, my boy," Spider laughed, "I predict this is the start of a wonderful friendship."

24